D0429043

KAY THOMPSON'S ELOISE

Eloise and the Very Secret Room

STORY BY Ellen Weiss

ILLUSTRATED BY Tammie Lyon

Ready-to-Read

Simon Spotlight
New York   London   Toronto   Sydney   New Delhi

My name is Eloise.
I am six.

I live on
the tippy-top floor
of The Plaza Hotel.

But I can go all over.

This is Skipperdee.
He wears sneakers.
Sometimes.

Skipperdee and I
like to take walks.

Here is what I like to do:
go down
that very, very,
long, long hall.

(It is the one that
goes past the room
with the stringy mops.)

There is a room
that is so secret
only I know about it.

Skipperdee and I, anyway.

It says LOST AND FOUND.

Maybe it is lost,
but I found it.

There are very good things in it.

If you tie a lot of
ties together,
you can jump rope.

It is also a good room
to spin in.

If we get tired,
we take a nap on a
fur coat.

Here is what else I can do:
wear nineteen hats.

A tennis racket makes
a very good turtle carrier.

I do not think anyone
has ever been in
this room but me.

It is a good room
to practice hollering in.

A hatbox makes a very
good drum.

In comes the manager.
"Eloise!" he says.
"Here you are!"

"Of course I am here,"
I say.
"Where else would I be?"

"We found you
    in the Lost and Found,"
says Nanny.

I was not lost at all.
I was right here
all the time.
Oooooooo I love, love, love
the Lost and Found.

Tomorrow I will see if that hat makes a good fishbowl.

KAY THOMPSON'S *ELOISE*

Eloise and the Dinosaurs

STORY BY **Lisa McClatchy**
ILLUSTRATED BY **Tammie Lyon**

Ready-to-Read

Simon Spotlight
New York   London   Toronto   Sydney   New Delhi

I am Eloise.
I am a city child.

I have a tutor.
His name is Philip.
He is boring, boring, boring.

Today
Philip is taking me
to the museum.

We are going
to see the dinosaurs.

Philip says,
"Here are the dinosaur halls!"

And he says,
"Please behave, Eloise."

And I say,
"Please behave, Eloise."

And he says,
"Here is a dinosaur."

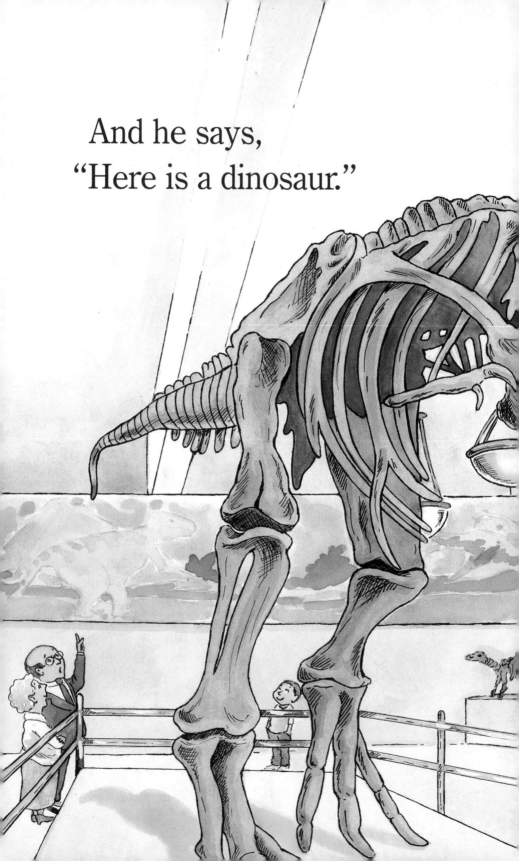

And I say,
"Here is a dinosaur."

Philip says,
"It is a Tyrannosaurus rex."

I say,
"It is a Tyrannosaurus rex."

Then he says,
"Please stop, Eloise."

Then I say,
"Please stop, Eloise."

And he says,
"Nanny, make her stop!"

Nanny says,
"No, no, no, Eloise!"

I skip over to
the triceratops.

My pink bow
looks just right
on his horn.

I cartwheel over to
the apatosaurus.

He needs a hat.

Philip says,
"Eloise, do not touch
the dinosaurs!"

Then Nanny says,
"Eloise,
  leave the dinosaurs alone.
  It is time for lunch."

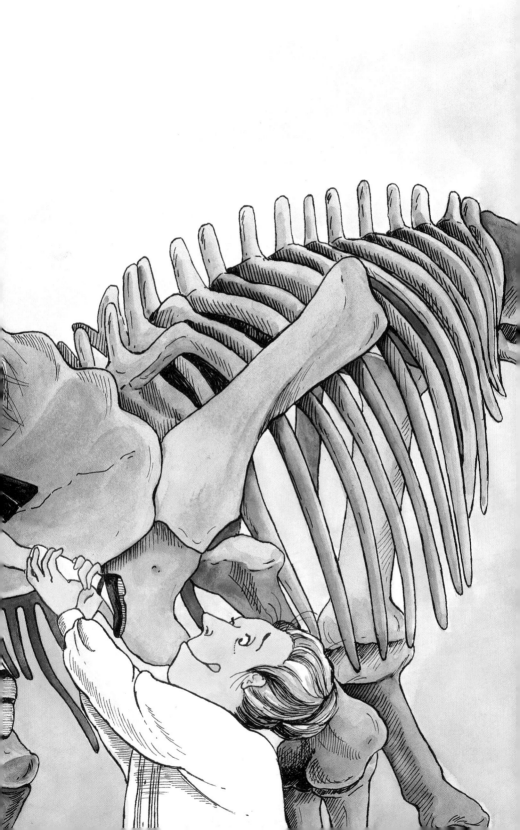

I say,
"Good-bye, dinosaurs."

Oh I love, love, love
dinosaurs!

KAY THOMPSON'S ELOISE

Eloise Has a Lesson

STORY BY **Margaret McNamara**

ILLUSTRATED BY **Kathryn Mitter**

Ready-to-Read

Simon Spotlight

New York   London   Toronto   Sydney   New Delhi

I am Eloise.
I am six.

I am a city child.

I live in a hotel
on the tippy-top floor.

This is Philip.

He is my tutor.
He is no fun.

Here is what I do not like:
doing math
for one half hour
in the morning.

Here is what I like:
teasing Philip.

Philip says, "Hello, Eloise."

I say, "Hello, Eloise."

Philip says, "Math time."

I say, "Bath time?"

Philip says, "Eloise, please."

I say, "Eloise, please."

Philip says,
"What is five plus six?"

I say, "You do not know?"

"Nanny!" says Philip.
"Make Eloise behave."
"Eloise, behave," says Nanny.

Chalk makes a very good straw.

"What is five plus six?"
says Philip.

"Five plus six is the same as six plus five," I say.

Philip says, "Oh, Eloise."

I say, "Oh, Eloise."

Nanny says,
"Math time is nearly over.

"Time to finish up, up, up."

Philip says, "Eloise."

I say, "Philip."

Philip says, "Think."

I say, "I am thinking."

Philip says,
"What is five plus six?"

"It is eleven," I say.
"And the lesson is over."

Oooooooooo,
I absolutely love math.

KAY THOMPSON'S ELOISE

Eloise's New Bonnet

STORY BY **Lisa McClatchy**

ILLUSTRATED BY **Tammie Lyon**

Ready-to-Read

Simon Spotlight

New York   London   Toronto   Sydney   New Delhi

I am Eloise.
I am six.
I live in The Plaza Hotel
on the tippy-top floor.

I have a dog.
His name is Weenie.

Here is what I like to do:
put sunglasses on Weenie.

Today the sun is shining.
Spring has sprung.
I put my sunglasses on too.

Nanny says, "Eloise,
you need a new hat."

Lampshades make
very good hats.

"No, no, no, Eloise,"
Nanny says.
"You need to find
a real hat."

"I know where to find
a real hat," I say.
"I will visit the kitchen."

Chef's hat makes
a very good hat.

"I know," I say. "I will visit room service."

Room service hats make very good hats.

"No, no, no, Eloise,"
Nanny says.
"That hat has no brim."

"Hmm," I say.
"I will visit
   the bell captain!"

Bell captain hats
make very good hats.

"No, no, no, Eloise," Nanny says.
"We need a hat that is a pretty color."

I visit the lobby.
There are hats everywhere!

I try on a lady's hat.
It is a pretty color,
and it has a bird on top.
"Perfect," I say.

Nanny and the manager
do not agree.

"Please give the lady
her hat back,"
Nanny says.

"Sorry."

"Eloise, I have a surprise,"
Nanny says.
She hands me a box.

Inside is a new hat
just for me.

Oh, I love, love, love hats!

KAY THOMPSON'S ELOISE

Eloise at the Wedding

STORY BY **Margaret McNamara**

ILLUSTRATED BY **Tammie Lyon**

Ready-to-Read

Simon Spotlight
New York   London   Toronto   Sydney   New Delhi

I am Eloise.
I live at The Plaza Hotel.

The Grand Ballroom
is busy today.

Cleaners are cleaning.

Cooks are cooking.

Waiters are waiting
for something to happen.

"What is going on?" I say.
"There will be
a wedding today,"
Nanny says.

"I am going," I say.
I love, love, love weddings.

"You are not going,"
Nanny says.
"No one has asked you
to go."

That is true.
No one has asked me.

Not yet.

"It is time for your bath,"
Nanny says.

In the bath I am:
a sea captain,

a mermaid,

the Statue of Liberty.

After the bath
I am clean, clean, clean.

Nanny says,
"If you are very good
you may see the bride."

I am as good as I can be.

We peek inside
the Grand Ballroom.
There are men
who look like penguins.

There are ladies
with large hats.

There is a groom.
There is no bride.

Nanny says, "Oh dear, oh dear, oh dear."

I hear a noise.
It is a sad noise.
It is a crying noise.

It is coming from
the powder room.
I look inside.

There is the bride.
She is crying.

"Oh dear, oh dear,
oh dear," she says.
"What is wrong?" I say.

"The flower girl is sick,"
she says.
"How can I get married?"

"Do you want me to be
   your flower girl?" I say.
"I do!" the bride says.

I am rather good
at being a flower girl.

Oooooooo I love, love, love weddings.

KAY THOMPSON'S ELOISE

Eloise Breaks Some Eggs

STORY BY Margaret McNamara

ILLUSTRATED BY Tammie Lyon

Ready-to-Read

Simon Spotlight
New York   London   Toronto   Sydney   New Delhi

I am Eloise.
I am six.

I am a city child.
I live in a hotel
on the tippy-top floor.

This is Nanny.

She is my nanny.
My mother is mostly away.

"Eloise," says Nanny.
"It is time for your lesson."

I ask, "Piano?"
Nanny says, "No."

I ask, "French?"
Nanny says, "No."

I ask, "Poker?"
Nanny says, "No, no, no."

"It is time for
your cooking lesson.

"Today you will cook eggs."

"I do not like to cook,"
I say.

"You like to break things,"
Nanny says.

"You break eggs
to cook them."

I say, "Let's go, go, go."

We take the elevator
to the kitchen.

I press every button.

"Today we will cook eggs,"
says the cook.

A bowl can make
a very good hat.
"No, no, no," says Nanny.

"Watch me," says the cook.
The cook is good.

"Now you try," he says.

I am very good.

"NO! NO! NO!" says Nanny.

"You broke the bowl!
You broke the plate!"
says the cook.

I say,
    "I broke the eggs, too."

Nanny and
I take the elevator
to the tippy-top floor.
I press every button.

"You will never be a cook,"
  says Nanny.
"How will you eat?"

I say, "Room service."
I pick up the phone.
I say, "It's me, Eloise.

"Two eggs,
    and charge it, please.
Thank you very much."